A Scottish Island Surprise

HOLLY WYLD

For my two sunbeams,
with all my love x

Author's Note

Dear Reader,

Welcome to Primrose Island!

I do so hope you enjoy meeting Rose as she grapples with the surprises that come to light on Primrose Island. Rose finds herself, in a very short space of time, journeying towards bringing herself 'home', letting down her barriers – and opening her heart to new friendships – and maybe, just maybe, to love...

I'm so glad to have you along, and I hope your heart is lifted by the warmth, humour and healing to be found in these stories.

If you enjoy your time on Primrose Island, be sure to keep an eye out for upcoming books in the series!

Finally, before I go, I have to tell you – it's true! In the far north of Scotland where I live – in a scattered handful of places like Caithness, Sutherland and Orkney (and, of course, on our very own Primrose Island) – we really do have blue primroses!

Love,

Holly x

Connect with Holly on Facebook!

www.facebook.com/authorhollywyld

Coffee.

Rose Mackie needed coffee. It didn't matter where in the world she woke up – in her London flat, or in some hotel in Copenhagen or Paris or New York – the first thoughts of the day were always coffee shaped.

And, it turned out, waking up this morning in a creaky old beach house somewhere in the Outer Hebrides was proving no different.

Coffee.

What was different in this instance, however, was the availability of said coffee.

Rose's photography commissions took her from one city to the next, one hotel to the next, all the year round – so getting a coffee fix first thing was usually no more complicated than making her way to the hotel lobby, or wandering outside to find some nice little street cafe.

Not the situation she was dealing with here.

She sighed and closed the last of the higgledy kitchen cupboards.

"There has to be a coffee pot in here somewhere," she murmured, drumming her fingers on the wooden counter, her eyes lingering briefly on the letter she'd received only two weeks earlier.

A house it had said. A house. In the Hebrides. Left to you by your father.

Who gets letters like that for goodness' sake? Not her. Well, not until two weeks ago.

As surprises went, it had been off-the-scale.

Rose had never dreamed that she would own an actual house. But it stung that it had come to her from her so-called father. Her whole life, the man had wanted nothing whatsoever to do with her – and yet here she was, standing in the middle of his creaky old seen-better-days kitchen for something... anything... that hinted at the possibility of some coffee.

She glanced around the kitchen again.

Up there?

There was a high shelf bracketed all the way around the room and laden with copper pots and pans.

Got to be worth a try. She'd looked everywhere else.

Had he been a coffee drinker, this Hector Mackie? This so-called father? The man in whose kitchen she now stood... Had he been a coffee fan, like her?

Rose shrugged.

Who knew. Her father's coffee habit – Hector Mackie's coffee habit – or lack of one, was just one of a long list of things she didn't know, and would never know, about him.

For a second, she tried to picture him. This man who'd wanted nothing to do with her. This man she would never now meet. She imagined him standing where she stood, in the same Scottish morning light. Imagined him walking from the table to the sink. His movements perhaps slow and measured. His eyes perhaps turning to the window and the driftwood-strewn beach. He'd look out to sea, perhaps, and maybe, just maybe he'd think about–

–No. Stop it, Rose told herself. Just stop it.

She closed her eyes.

The feeling was back again. The feeling she couldn't name, and didn't want to name, twisting inside her. Gnawing and scratching and hurting. She exhaled and pushed it away and buried it with all the other feelings she had no use for.

Coffee.

She chose a solid-looking chair and dragged it across the floor, positioning it under the copper-laden shelf. She had her right foot squared on it before she realised she was no longer alone. Slowly, she turned.

Mismatched eyes. A salt and pepper coat. And a lolling pink tongue.

Chapter Two

"What the–"

Joe Fraser's heart clutched and his wire-cutters sprang from his fingers when he heard the scream. He swore under his breath, vaulted the stock fence he was repairing, and burst into a sprint across the still-wet grass towards Hector's place.

Moments later he was breathing hard in the doorway of Hector Mackie's kitchen, his eyes clamped on the woman he knew at once to be the man's daughter.

Same dark hair – hers a glossy tumble falling about her shoulders. Same storm-filled eyes.

She was standing on a chair, in just about enough cotton and lace, bathed in soft morning light.

Joe felt his heart clutch for the second time that morning.

She was beautiful.

She was also terrified.

RUFF!

Coll. Hector's dog. Now unofficially Joe's dog.

If Joe had this woman pegged as a Mackie the moment he laid eyes on her, the scruffy border collie that was evidently the source of the woman's distress obviously agreed.

The dog was blinking benignly – nope, adoringly – at her. Tongue lolling. Tail thumping.

RUFF!

Joe chuckled. Aye. Apparently, Coll knew a Mackie when he saw one, too.

"Miss?" Joe began, hoping to shed some light on the situation.

"Shhhh..." The woman raised a shaky finger to her lips. "We don't want to startle it."

Though her voice was uneven, and no louder than a whisper, Joe could hear the cut-glass Englishness in it.

"Miss, the thing is..." Joe started up again, taking a step closer – until he saw her stiffen, at which point he stopped in his tracks.

"It's okay," he murmured, dropping his voice instinctively. "Old Coll here would never hurt you."

Joe saw the woman dart a wary look at him. Weighing her options. Deciding whether to trust him or not. And he felt a twist of something. A deep pang in his belly. A man could lose all–

He cut the thought down.

Forget what a man could lose in those eyes.

They were pretty eyes, that was all. She had pretty eyes.

The woman flicked her attention from him to the dog – and back to him again.

"Rabies," she whispered. "Is rabies a possibility?"

Joe barked out an involuntary laugh. "Rabies?"

"Yes," said the woman, a little put out by his mockery. "Rabies."

Joe scrubbed a hand over his face.

Rabies.

Granted, Coll wasn't the most conventional or, if he were honest, the most appealing-looking dog. He had odd-coloured eyes that didn't quite line up, and a way of tilting his head that lent him a slightly manic look. But that was all surface level. Deep down, old Coll was soft as butter and as loyal as they came.

"Far as I'm aware–" Joe said, dropping his head briefly, the better to compose his features, "–far as I'm aware, Miss, we've no rabies in the Hebrides at the moment."

"Rose," she said, fixing another dubious look on the dog. "I'm Rose."

Joe smiled. "Rose. I guessed, aye. I'm Joe. Look, I know Coll here's a bit daft-looking. But honestly, he's friendly. He's one of the good ones."

"You're sure?" she said, her eyes flicking from the dog to him. "You're absolutely sure?"

"Aye. I'm sure," Joe said with another long low chuckle as he reached down to ruffle the collie's ears.

"He belonged to your fa–" Joe began, but then paused and straightened and rephrased. "He belonged to Hector."

Chapter Three

Her father.

"Really?" Rose said, watching the collie about-turn and skitter across the bare boards of the kitchen and lope off through the open door towards the beach. "He was my father's dog? Hector's, I mean..." She felt a sudden forlorn reluctance to see the old dog go.

"Don't worry," Joe said, as if he'd read her mind. "He'll be back."

Rose took the opportunity at this point to look properly at this Joe person. This man who'd come running when he'd heard her scream.

He was six foot something. All jean's and boots and an old checked shirt. A face that was all handsome planes and angles. She noticed that his eyes were very dark. Maybe even a little sad. She also noticed that they were being politely averted.

Why was he averting– *Wait...*

Rose glanced down at herself.

Oh no. *Oh NO!* A sudden deep blush started in her toes and proceeded steadily north. Not only had she just behaved like an idiot. She was also not really wearing very much.

Inclining her head, pressing her lips together, striving for dignity though there wasn't a whole lot to be had, Rose made a move to step down from the chair.

With a couple of long strides, Joe closed the distance between them and offered her his hand while still managing to – mostly, thankfully – avert his gaze.

Rose opened her mouth, on the point of refusing, on the point of saying something. But no words came. Instead, she felt his fingers close around hers, and she became very aware of the way their eyes locked for a moment – Joe holding her gaze while he helped her down.

"Thanks," she said, pulling her hand away and edging a little away from him.

Joe himself took a step backwards, opening up some space between them, hooking his thumbs into his jeans.

"You okay?" he said quietly.

"Yes. Sorry. You must think I'm an idiot. I mean, I am an idiot. Obviously."

"No. I don't think that."

Rose heard herself laugh nervously. "It's just that, I suppose I'm a bit out of my comfort zone, and–"

Joe kept his eyes level with hers and she could see now, even though she was inching away from him, that they were a very dark blue.

"–and yes, when I saw it, when I saw the dog – Coll?– I just..." She shrugged. "For some reason, rabies was the first thing that popped into my head. Rabies! In Scotland! Ridiculous, right?"

She clasped her hands together in front of her and continued backing away from Joe. "I've been on the road for a while, I suppose. I'm a photographer–"

"Hector told me, aye."

That threw her. "Wh– *He did?*"

Joe smiled. "Aye. He did."

"Oh. Well, yes, photography... I spend a lot of time on the road, and..."

She was gabbling. Why was she gabbling? She never gabbled.

"...Gosh, I've just been so busy and..." Rose paused briefly. Was it fifteen? Had she chalked up fifteen cities and as many hotels in the last month alone?

It wouldn't surprise her.

Six days ago she'd woken up in Tokyo convinced she was in Paris, only to discover after a series of very confusing phone calls that she was, in fact, in Istanbul. That didn't really qualify as busy, now that she thought about it. Really, it just qualified as bonkers.

"...and, yes," she picked up again. "A lot has been going on..."

Joe continued to watch her, as if any moment now her rambling might actually yield some sort of sense.

"I–" Rose allowed her voice to trail off and then she just offered him a weak smile.

Joe smiled a slow smile back at her.

"I think what I'm trying to say is..." she heard her voice waver the tiniest bit. "I think I might be quite tired."

Joe folded his arms. He was still looking at her. Still studying her intently. "Don't worry about it," he said quietly. Kindly, even. "Long as you're okay."

She smiled at him. "I'm Rose. Did I mention that?"

Joe nodded. Smiled back. "You did."

"Right. And you're Joe...?"

"Joe Fraser."

"Fraser..." Rose recognised the name from the paperwork she'd been advised to look at.

"As in, Joe Fraser, mentioned in Hector's will?"

Joe nodded. "So I'm told. I was Hector's nearest neighbour," Joe said. "Couple of miles along the beach there," he indicated over his shoulder. "We were friends," he added, a small muscle tensing along his jaw.

"Right," Rose said. "Well, we should probably, you know, talk then. Should we?"

Joe was still looking at her very intently.

"Aye," he said. "We should. Things might be more complicated than you–"

"I'll just –" Rose interrupted. She closed her eyes for a second, then flashed an apologetic smile at him. "I'll just put some clothes on first."

Chapter Four

Joe stood in Hector's cosy old kitchen listening to the strangely intimate sound of Rose Mackie's bare feet padding lightly down the hall. He exhaled a long, slow breath.

So *that* was Hector's daughter. *That* was Rose.

There was a pack of unopened coffee lying on the counter. He opened it, then unhooked his old friend's coffee pot from above the range, like he'd done a hundred times. As if nothing had changed. As if Hector were still alive. He unscrewed it and heaped in the rich-smelling grounds.

Had it only been a month? It seemed unreal. Joe still felt as though his old pal could walk through the door, laughing one of his deep laughs. Clapping him heavily on the back.

Hector had had things on his mind. Joe knew that much. Something had been bothering him. But Hector was always way too stubborn to ask for help. He'd been a loner through and through. Lived that way. And died that way, too, in the end.

Joe glanced out the window and traced the rise of the wildflower hill that overlooked the bay.

That's where they'd found him. His heart had given out.

Joe screwed the coffee pot together and lit the flame under it.

This. Hector's daughter being here. *Rose* being here. It was hard to swallow. Because Hector had wanted so much to meet her. Had wanted so much to put things right. And now… Now that he was *dead* – here she was.

Chapter Five

Rose closed the door of the bathroom adjoining the bedroom she'd slept in the night before, and plunged her face into her hands.

How embarrassing. How unbelievably embarrassing.

Gah. What a meltdown! What on earth had all that been about? She was at the top of her field. Thought nothing of organising high-profile exhibitions, directing photography shoots, handling the egos and agendas of more difficult clients than she cared to count… So why the blathering idiot routine in front of Mr Checked Shirt?

She shook her head, turned on the shower taps, and stepped under the soft warm spray.

She was jet-lagged, and she longed for a bath. But she'd have to make do. Too many cities in too few days, that was the problem. And too many five-minute showers, she thought, as she quickly lathered and rinsed shampoo out of her hair. She'd perfected it over the years, the whole five-minute thing.

Or maybe she had just perfected being permanently rushed.

The funny thing was, when she was twenty and just starting out, she'd imagined that being a photographer would be a slow-paced sort of career. A relaxed, bohemian pace. A relaxed, bohemian life. But now, nearly two decades later, her life was anything *but* slow – and anything *but* bohemian.

What did it mean to pine for a life that was gentler, attuned to the seasons – attuned to nature – when all you really knew, all you really lived, was airport terminals and hotel rooms?

Rose frowned. It meant that you were unrealistic, she thought, pushing all thoughts of romantic rural idylls from her mind.

She wrapped herself in a towel and hurried through to the bedroom. At least this unexpected week in the Outer Hebrides would give her a chance to catch her breath. Even if she did have a house to empty, a briefcase full of paperwork to sign off, and a buyer to find. It would still be a holiday compared with the usual madness.

She dressed quickly in a pair of jeans and her favourite old cardigan, pausing briefly at the small wall mirror to twist her still-damp hair into a bun. And then, she closed her eyes and took a long, deep inhale.

Coffee...

"Hi. Again," she said as she walked back into the kitchen. She felt suddenly, oddly shy – but at least a lot less foolish now that she was wearing clothes.

Joe lifted his head and gave her a sideways smile, and a little hitch of his eyebrows.

"Ah. You found the coffee pot," said Rose. "I had no such luck."

"Aye," Joe said. "It lives there." He nodded at a well-placed hook above the stove.

"Ah."

"Hope you don't mind. Thought you could use a cup."

"Like you wouldn't believe."

Chapter Six

Joe handed Rose her coffee and studied the contents of his own cup for a moment. Then he levelled his gaze at her. "I wanted to say that I'm sorry. About your father. He was a good man."

Rose froze. Felt her blood cool. Her stomach tighten.

A good man? Was a man who dumped his pregnant fiancée and sent her away *a good man?* Was a guy who denied the existence of the child he'd fathered *a good man?* Call her old fashioned, but in her opinion, her father – Hector, she corrected herself for the umpteenth time – was not, and never had been, a good man.

"That's debatable, Joe," she said quietly, brushing past him, moving to the large casement window that looked out onto the sea.

"I'm sorry?" said Joe, following her to the window.

Rose felt a tremor go through her, and rubbed her arms in an attempt to banish it. She couldn't figure out whether it was all this talk of her father, or all this cool Scottish sea air – or just the proximity of this... this Joe Fraser person... but being here was making her feel rattled and spiky and... more unsettled than she had envisaged, frankly.

"I said that's debatable..."

A shadow came over Joe's face. A shadow, or something approaching indignation, she realised. She felt a sudden need to explain.

"My father didn't give a damn about me, Joe," she said. She looked straight at him, aware once again that her voice sounded unsteady.

A faded, unwanted memory drifted into her mind. Of herself. On her eleventh birthday. Of how she'd waited all day long for the doorbell to ring – convinced that her father would magically appear that day to claim her as his daughter. That she and her mother and her father would live happily ever after. That she wouldn't have to stay at boarding school. That they would be a family. She sank her nails into her palms, willing away the tears that threatened even now, even after all these years. She'd wasted too much time on daydreams. Had cried too many tears over a man who simply hadn't cared.

"And–" she, went on, swallowing hard, fighting for composure. "And I haven't come here to moon around in this beach house pretending that I'm sorry he's..." She paused. Took an extra breath, "...that I'm sorry he's dead. Because the truth of the matter is..." Her throat felt horribly tight. Say it, Rose. Just say it. Say it. Own it. And accept it. "The truth of the matter is, I was nothing to him. And the sooner all the paperwork is finalised and I can clear this house and get out of here... The better."

Joe was glaring at her. She didn't care. She suddenly just needed it all to be over. Needed to consign all of it to the past. Needed, desperately, to move on.

"I would appreciate it if we could just get on with whatever it is we're supposed to be getting on with."

Rose barely recognised her own voice. It sounded odd and strained and far away. It sounded, she realised, cold. But she wouldn't give ground. She set her mouth. And she matched his stare, waiting for him to say something, absorbing the details of his hard mouth, his dark features. Even his body, his posture, was somehow straighter. Harder. Evidently she had shocked him, or angered him. But what right did he have to be shocked? To be angry? He didn't know the first thing about any of it. Or about her.

An uncomfortable silence settled between them, and they continued to stare at one another.

"You're wrong," Joe said, eventually, shifting away from the counter. His voice was low and steady.

Of all the arrogant... Indignation flared in Rose's cheeks. *Who did this Joe Fraser think he was?*

"Wrong?" she spluttered. "I'm *wrong?* I'm sorry, Mr Fraser, but I think I have a better idea than you what, if anything, my father felt for me."

That was putting it mildly. She'd been on the receiving end of nothing for thirty-six years.

Chapter Seven

Joe rubbed his jaw for a moment, taking the situation in. Taking *her* in. The eyes, indignant, glittering with anger. The cheeks, stained pink. The mouth, stubborn. He knew that package. Beautiful. Stylish. Cold. Break a man's heart wide open as easily as choose a new pair of shoes.

He'd been there and done that.

He set his cup down hard, sloshing coffee onto the table.

"Sorry, Miss Mackie. But I don't think you do."

"Really? And how would– " Rose started to challenge him, but it was too late. He'd already turned his back on her. He was leaving.

Eyes wide, brow creased, and mouth slightly open, Rose followed his long strides to the door, watching as he stopped abruptly and muttered something she didn't hear before turning to face her again.

"My folks..." he said, his voice flat. His eyes dark and empty. "They've invited you over for dinner tonight..."

He was half way out the door before he threw over his shoulder: "Pick you up at seven."

Rose's mouth fell open all the way. He was joking, wasn't he? He had to be absolutely *joking?*

Chapter Eight

"Unbelievable," Rose muttered, clearing the cups and coffee pot to the sink. Simply unbelievable. As if she didn't have enough to deal with right now. The last thing she needed from Joe Fraser – co-named in Hector's will for goodness' sake – was a guilt trip.

A guilt trip he had no right to lay on her.

She tutted and shook her head again, as if doing so would also shake the man from her thoughts.

"Sorry, Mr Fraser," she said, running water into the sink and adding a squirt of washing up liquid. "But you can shove your guilt trip. And you can shove your dinner invite, too."

She had a house to empty – and less than a week to do it in.

Chapter Nine

Rose eventually decided on a plan of attack. She would allocate half a day to each room for boxing and sorting, and that would leave her a couple of days to iron out any admin or paperwork.

Could she have done this remotely? By proxy? Probably. It wasn't like she needed the stress. She had plenty of that already. But she'd wanted to see the house. On some level she'd needed to see it. And since she'd planned to come, it had made sense that she would also clear it and get it ready for sale.

Her walk round had given her a pretty good feel for the place. It was old, but well loved. Her father's folk, *her folk*, she supposed, had clearly been long of the island.

By the look of it, and from what she'd unearthed from the bits of paperwork she'd pulled together, the original part of the house had been one simple room constructed with stones pulled off the beach. And in generations since, sections and another floor had been added.

She touched one of the walls. To think her ancestors had built it. To think their *hands* had made it.

A shiver went through her.

She stood there, taking it in. Wondering about the stories and secrets, the joys and the heartbreaks, the births and the deaths this home had seen. To think that she had a connection, albeit a distant one, with all those stories. All those lives.

She wandered through to the sitting room next, and placed another log on the fire. She had to admit, for a cold man, Hector's house certainly had a warmth to it. The comfortable furniture. Books and paintings and interesting objects. She hadn't expected to like it so much. Hadn't expected to like it at all, really. But she did. She liked its homeliness and its easy style.

There was a small study off the sitting room, and as she continued through to it something brushed past her legs and made her jump.

She didn't entirely relax when she saw that it was the weird-eyed dog. *Coll.*

"You again..." Rose stopped in her tracks and stayed where she was, eyeing him carefully for signs of feral behaviour. But he just ambled across the room to a comfy old armchair that faced the fireplace and slumped at the foot of it.

Rose felt a lump come to her throat. *Her father's chair.*

"You miss him," she heard herself say, and she crossed the room towards the dog, crouching down to get a closer look.

He just lay there. Meek and mute and still. His head resting on his paws. His eyes all big and sad.

"Poor old thing," she murmured, stroking his head gently. "You're really quite nice, aren't you? I'll tell you what. You have a nap there while I get started on these boxes. Just between the two of us, I'd be glad of the company."

She left Coll to his dozing and went to the pile of flat-pack boxes she'd stacked by the bookshelves. Wrestling one of them into a box shape – bending and slotting until she had it strong and square – she scanned the first set of shelves. It was mostly given over to books on plants and wildlife. One of the volumes caught her eye though – a gold-edged leather-bound edition – and she pulled it from the shelf. *Flora and Fauna of the Outer Hebrides.* There was an inscription inside the cover, penned in a sloping, elegant hand.

For Hector. Happy twenty-first birthday, son. With fondest love, Mother and Father.

"Oh my goodness..." she murmured, tracing a finger lightly over the words. Her grandparents. Her grandmother's handwriting.

From nowhere, Rose felt tears spill onto her cheeks. She brushed them away and snapped the book shut.

This felt wrong. Could she do this? Could she box up his life like this?

Without... Without what? She blew out a breath. Put the heels of her hands to her eyes for several moments. This house, the books, his things. They were the last link. The last real connection to the man she'd spent her whole life longing to meet. He might not have wanted to know her, but if this was her last chance to get some sense of who he was, of what he was like... Would she regret not taking advantage of it? If she boxed everything up and gave everything away, what then? What would be left of him? Her mother was gone, so this really was it. Her last chance to find out something about him.

And possibly her last chance to find out something about herself.

She went to the window and looked out across the water. Some air would be good, she realised. And she could take her camera, get a few captures. Maybe try and figure out if she could squeeze any more days out of her schedule while she was at it.

Back in the kitchen, she pulled on her cardigan and looped her camera over her shoulder, stopping in her tracks just before she pulled the door closed behind her. Should she invite him? Would he come?

"Coll?" she called into the house. And for several seconds, she heard nothing. But then there was a scuffle of paws in the hall, quickly followed by the sight of Hector's dog barrelling into the kitchen. Rose grinned and bent to ruffle his ears.

"Shall we?"

Chapter Ten

Joe straightened and stretched his back, moving his neck side to side, easing out the tension. The light was dying out of the sky. It'd be getting towards seven by now.

Weary, grim-faced, he threw a tangle of wire and a bunch of broken fence posts into the back of his truck. Neighbourliness. Generosity. Kindness. Social niceties. The cornerstones of his folks' lives. The trouble he'd be in if he didn't bring Hector's girl to dinner tonight.

He gunned the engine. He was annoyed. And mainly with himself. Things were off to a bad start with Rose, and that was down to him. He'd spoken out of turn this morning. Should have remembered he didn't know the full story. And though she'd wanted nothing to do with Hector, she was likely grieving, in her own way.

He hung a hard left towards the old beach house. Thoughts turning back to Rose and her late father. He stood by what he said. She *was* wrong. The fact was, Hector *had* cared. If he hadn't cared, why would he have collected all those clippings about her? All those prints of her work? And how could he have reeled off all the cities she'd ever been to?

Joe shook his head. He'd asked Hector once, asked him why the two of them had never met. But Hector had just made it known in his own quiet way that the subject was closed. Anyway. Whatever the story was, he'd apologise. And then he'd get on with seeing that Hector's wishes for the house were seen to. That's what Hector had asked of him. That's what he would do. Beyond that, he needed to get his mind back on his own responsibilities. Like Sam.

He drove for a couple of miles, deep in thought, until the vision of a slight, dark-haired figure on the road ahead pulled him up short. Rose? He squinted into the dusk. Yeah, it was her. And if that wasn't Coll, scampering along beside her. Joe gave a low chuckle, feeling his mood lighten. They looked like they'd become friends. And maybe he felt a pang of something about that. He pulled himself up on it though. He'd easily have fallen for Rose at one point. Not now though. He had people – and more specifically a little boy – counting on him. There'd be no friendship with Rose Mackie. No friendship. No nothing.

"No," he murmured to himself, lowering the window as he gained on Rose and the dog. "It'll be better for both of us of, Rose, when the wind blows you back to wherever it was it blew you in from..."

Joe slowed his truck. Fixed a neighbourly smile on his face. "Evening..."

Chapter Eleven

Rose threw a glance over her shoulder and her stomach caved. *Drat*. Him. In a truck. Smiling at her.

"Oh. It's you. Hello." She flickered a brief look at him without slowing her pace, and settled her eyes back on the road ahead. Not that her reluctance to stop and chat seemed to faze him. He just slowed the truck to a crawl, and followed along beside her. Annoyingly amused, apparently. And annoyingly handsome.

"Hope you weren't planning on skipping our date?" Joe said.

Rose darted a quick look at him, saw a glint of mischief in his eyes. *Date*. As if. But anyway, full marks Joe. That's exactly what she'd been planning. She hadn't refined the details, but she'd broadly envisaged that it would involve hiding behind, or under, a sizeable rock at around the time Joe would be calling. But–thwarted. And so to Plan B.

Talking her way out of it.

"Skipping our date? Mr Fraser, I would never skip out on a date unless there were extenuating circumstances. Remarkably, however, tonight is one of those rare situations, and I'm afraid I have to–"

Joe held up a hand. "Uh-uh. No. Nope. I'm going to stop you right there, Rose. I'm not sure you understand. This is not optional. My life won't be worth living if I don't deliver you into my mother's lair tonight."

He reached across the passenger seat and pushed the door open. Flashed another mischief-loaded smile at her.

"And, frankly, neither will yours. Come on now," he said, still smiling, "do the decent thing."

Rose fought the urge to swear. She *so* did not want to have dinner with this man, or any of his blood relations.

Droplets of rain started to spatter around her.

Great. As if her options weren't narrow enough. It was looking increasingly likely that she would have to capitulate.

"But I've the dog with me," she tried, a last-ditch effort, underpinned by the sinking feeling that having Coll with her would get her out of exactly nothing.

Joe splayed his hands, his smile widening.

"Coll's like family to us..."

Rose glared at him. "Of course he is. How silly of me."

Then she rolled her eyes and clambered into the passenger seat.

Chapter Twelve

Taking a deep, fortifying breath Rose followed Joe to the front door of his cottage.

His parents were standing there waiting for them. And while she'd never bought in to her own mother's obsession with appearances, Rose did, at least, pride herself on decent manners.

She walked up the steps towards them, smiling what she hoped was an acceptably gracious smile.

"Rose, my father, Robert. My mother, Mary. They live on the other side of the island. But any excuse to gatecrash here. Especially now we've got wee Sam to keep us busy."

"Lovely to meet you, Mr and Mrs Fraser. Thank you so much for inviting me to dinner."

"Welcome to Primrose Island, dear. And please accept our sympathies. Your father was a fine man."

Rose looked at the ground, grateful that Coll skirted around her legs just then, closely followed by a dark-haired little boy whom Joe caught and scooped into his arms.

"And this, Rose," he said, by way of explanation, "is Sam. Our all-round right-hand man. Couldn't run the place without him."

The little boy's face lit up, and his chest puffed out proudly. *Joe's son?* Rose wondered, feeling at the same time a sharp little squeeze in her chest.

Mary leaned towards her, as if reading her mind. "Joe's godson," she said in a hushed tone. "Parents are, you know..." Mary lifted her eyes heavenwards. Joe is his guardian. We help out best we can."

Mary pushed her hands into her floral apron and beamed lovingly at the sight of Joe dangling the boy by his ankles and swinging him from left to right.

"Joe's just wonderful with him."

"Oh, I–" Rose wasn't sure what she wanted to say. Whatever it was, the words lodged in her throat, and stayed there.

Robert ushered all of them inside and Joe set the little boy on his feet again. "Sam, you'll take care of Coll, won't you?" he said to the boy.

Sam nodded importantly.

"As for you, Rose, I will leave you in my mother's capable hands while I go and clean up a bit."

Rose had a random, unbidden thought that he looked just fine as he was. She caught that rogue thought – and trampled it.

Mary took her through to the kitchen, and explained they would be eating in there.

"It's nothing fancy, dear. We just wanted to welcome you. Say hello."

"You're very kind." Rose nodded at the huge casserole pot keeping warm on top of the range. Smells great."

Mary beamed at her. Rose guessed that Joe had her eyes.

Soon enough Joe reappeared in clean jeans and t-shirt. His hair still damp from the shower.

"Come on folks. Let's eat," said Robert. He had the same low-timbre voice as his son. "And you Rose, I want you to eat plenty, please. You look like you can't weigh more than a bag of oats."

Rose raised her eyebrows and stifled a laugh. But a few mouthfuls in, she was more than happy enough to oblige. The food was delicious.

The Frasers chatted and laughed and told stories and talked about the early winter that was coming. It was easy and comfortable. Warm. *This*, Rose thought, *this* was what families did.

"Mrs Fraser, that was delicious," Rose said when Joe's mother began to clear the plates.

"Mary, sweetheart. Call me Mary."

Rose smiled. She liked this woman.

Rose looked across the table at Joe. The way his mouth was tugging at the corners. He was clearly tickled by her temporary shelving of hostilities. At least as far as his mother was concerned.

She narrowed her eyes at him, only to see him smile a slow, wicked smile back at her, before leaning back in his chair and clasping his hands behind his head – the very picture of the sated, contended male.

Infuriating. He was infuriating. Too handsome. And yes, really quite infuriating. And yet... Every time she'd looked at him throughout dinner, he'd somehow been looking back at her. And each time their eyes had locked, butterflies had fluttered in her tummy.

That being the case, she studiously avoided his eyes for the entire duration of the apple pie and coffee course.

"Rose?"

A small voice sounded at her left elbow. Sam. Joe's godson. He had slid off his chair and scooted around the table to where she was. He didn't look a lot older than five.

"Oh. Hello." Rose said. She hadn't had much experience with children.

"How many freckles have I got?" he said, his little face all solemn and serious.

"How many... how many *freckles?*" she said, taking a sip of wine to disguise her smile. Then she set down her glass and shifted slightly so that they were facing each other properly.

"Hmmm," she said, "let me see..." She creased her brow and peered into his little face, moving her lips and murmuring numbers to herself. "One hundred and seventy-six," she announced at last. Then she tipped his chin gently and added. "No. Wait. One hundred and seventy-seven."

Sam laughed loudly, his seriousness gone, an ear-to-ear smile in its place.

"Do you like stories?" he demanded.

"I love stories. How did you know?"

"Want to see my favourite book?"

Rose smiled warmly at him. "You bet I do..."

Sam raced off in search of a book, a blur of curls and stripes and odd socks. He was adorable.

She laughed quietly and brought her glass to her lips again. As she did so, she saw that Joe was watching her again, this time with a curious half smile on his face. Then he got up and cleared some plates away to the sink.

Before he could even reach for the tap, Mary bustled towards him and batted his hand away, clucking her tongue at him and shooting him a reprimanding look. "No. You already do too much. Away from there." She snapped her tea towel at him in mock annoyance and, towering over her, Joe chuckled and planted a kiss on her head. Mary smiled. "I said away!"

Rose felt her heart squeeze. She couldn't put into words why having dinner with this family, why watching these easy domestic scenes unfold around her made her feel somehow happy and comfortable, and at the same time, somehow... unbearably sad. It was obvious that Joe adored his family. And obvious that they adored him. It was that simple. That lovely.

He was lovely. Wait. No. *He* was infuriating.

Rose closed her eyes, and pressed her fingers to her temples. Good grief, she was so jet-lagged.

"Rose." His low voice, the way he said her name. It sent something whispering along her spine. She opened her eyes and found that he was looking at her again.

"You're tired. Come on. I'll take you home."

Home. Her throat constricted, and the feeling stole over her again. The empty, aching feeling.

"Right. Yes, I am a bit tired actually."

She turned away from him quickly, scooping her cardigan off the back of her chair, praying that he hadn't noticed the tears pricking at her eyes.

Quick little footsteps came up behind her.

"You can take this one home with you."

It was Sam. He thrust a dog-eared picture book into her hands. There were three owls on the front cover. Rose might not know the first thing about children, but she recognised a much-loved possession when she saw one.

"Are you sure, Sam? This looks like it might be a very special book..."

Sam nodded. "It's my favourite."

Rose felt her heart tug, and had to fight off an urge to pull him into her arms and squeeze him. She crouched down and looked him in the eye and took his little hands in hers instead. "Then I will treasure it, Sam," she said softly. And she meant it.

Chapter Thirteen

Rose said her thank yous and goodbyes to Mary and Robert and Sam, and felt three pairs of eyes follow her and Joe into the darkness and towards his truck.

Joe held the passenger door open for her.

"Thanks," she said. "Thanks for a lovely evening."

She suddenly felt oddly shy. It *had* been a lovely evening, despite her earlier misgivings. And, yes, it was just another supper to the Frasers. But to her, the whole event had been nothing short of revelatory. She'd never really experienced the sort of cosy domesticity that she'd felt around her, and been a part of, tonight.

Her own mother had been proudly unmaternal, if not completely indifferent to her. And along the way, some part of Rose had absorbed the idea that she herself would never be *mother material* either. And certainly, Lawrence, her ex, hadn't wanted children.

But just now, with Joe's godson, she had felt the strongest stirring she'd ever felt that... actually maybe she *would* like to be a mother one day. It occurred to her suddenly that not only had no one ever asked her what her thoughts were on that. She'd also never even figured out herself what those thoughts might be.

Tonight, though... Tonight, she'd felt a vague sort of stirring. A vague sort of sense that there was a lot of that kind of love in her heart. She just hadn't yet found the right person – or people – to give it to.

Her mind circled back to the Frasers' easy warmth. The fierce bonds that bound them. The fierce love that underpinned their lives.

And then she thought about herself. About her own life. About how she'd reached her mid-thirties, and was beginning to feel the patterns and routines of her life firming up.

She had sat there in the Frasers' kitchen tonight and realised that her life was forming into a lonely shape.

She dragged her mind off the past, and off herself, and turned it back to Joe. He'd swung behind the wheel, and was smiling at her.

"Glad you enjoyed it," he said, turning his truck onto the winding track that would take them back to Hector's beach cottage.

Her tummy fluttered again, and she fixed her eyes on the star-lit stretch of road ahead of them.

They drove a mile or so in silence, and Rose found herself wondering if it was possible to fall in love with someone in the space of a few hours.

Ridiculous. She must be losing her marbles. Only a few hours had passed since she was silently cursing him.

"Rose..." It was Joe who cut through the quiet. "About this morning..."

She glanced at him but he was keeping his gaze straight. "I was out of line there – and I want to apologise for that."

Rose began to fidget with a bracelet on her wrist. "Please don't. Apologise, I mean. It was me. I don't know, I'm a bit strung out right now. Or on a short fuse. Or just jet-lagged..."

"I still apologise."

They glanced at each other and exchanged shy smiles.

"And I'm just relieved that you're okay with, you know, the clause thing."

"Clause thing?"

Joe darted a look at her.

"What clause? What clause, Joe?"

"The clause, Rose," said Joe. "The clause in Hector's will that–"

"Oh no," he murmured, scanning her face the best he could while also paying due attention to the road, especially since it had started to rain heavily.

"So you don't know yet."

"What don't I know, Joe? I'm lost..."

Another darted look from him. Arguably a very apologetic one.

"I'm sorry," he said. "You shouldn't be hearing it from me. Hector put a clause in his will... a clause that... well, that..."

"That *what*, Joe? A clause that WHAT!?"

A muscle worked along his jaw and he kept his eyes straight ahead on the road this time. "A clause that requires me to approve the buyer of Hector's house."

"Oh. My. God." Now Rose stared – numb, suddenly – at the road ahead.

"And if I don't agree?" she said flatly, something, some intuition telling her this wasn't going to be good.

"Well, aye. In that case, you would have to... stay on the island for a full year."

"WHAT!?"

"–Before you could sell it to, you know, whoever you wanted to sell it to."

"Oh my GOD! Stop the car!"

"Rose, I'm–"

"I said, stop the car!"

"Rose. It's pouring with rain. You can't–"

"I am perfectly fine with rain, thank you."

"Let me take you to the house."

"Stop the car NOW."

Joe stopped the car and leaned close to her, closer still and closer even still.

Rose froze, and realised she was holding her breath. Realised she was waiting. But for what? For him to... *for him to k–*

–No! She extinguished the thought. But he continued to lean towards her, and suddenly time slowed and everything telescoped, and there was just the rough graze of his bare arm glancing past hers, the lightest brush of his fingers against the fabric of her blouse as he... reached past her and clunked open the passenger side door.

For the merest fraction of a second, before he moved away, Joe held his position and their eyes locked – the same way they had during dinner. *What was happening?* Was this–

Coll at that moment however leapt between them from the back seats and scrabbled over Rose's lap in order to squeeze himself out of the widening door gap.

Good. It brought her to her senses.

She had no business – NO business whatsoever – entertaining the idea of kissing Joe Fraser. She wasn't some daft sixteen-year-old.

She pushed the door open further and stepped out into the sheeting rain.

She gulped. *Wow – oh, okay – yes, this was rain.* Not unlike having someone repeatedly throw buckets of water into one's face.

She gulped again, and wrapped her already sodden cardigan tightly around herself.

"Fine!"

Joe's voice, behind her.

"Have it your way. But I'm walking you back."

She heard him drop into a steady stride a few paces behind her.

Walking her back? She threw a half-look over her shoulder. *Stalking* her back, more like.

Gosh, though. It was dark. No such thing as light pollution here. And the crashing of the waves seemed louder too. Rose was suddenly incredibly glad to see the little blinking porch light of her cottage – Hector's cottage – half a mile or so ahead of her.

And as annoying as he undoubtedly was – and although it pained her hugely to admit it – Rose was in fact quite glad that Joe was a few steps behind her.

"We're going to have to find a way to work together on this," he called through the battering rain. "I didn't put that clause in Hector's will. This isn't my fault!" he shouted over the increasingly loud roar of the waves. "And I don't know why he did it!"

Rose stopped power walking and swung around to face him. Her unexpected about-turn caused them a moment of brief collision – and Rose found herself with her hands splayed against his wide strong chest, and – worse – an unfathomable reluctance to remove them.

But remove them she did.

"Fine," she shouted over the crashing waves. "But what IS your fault is– is–"

What *was* his fault, exactly?

"OH NEVER MIND?" she yelled, adding, "And thank you for the

meal. You've no idea how glad I am we have ticked *that* box and I shall have no further obligation to spend any time with you whatsoever!"

"Rose..." Joe called after her, Rose having resumed her soggy stomping towards the cottage. "Rose!"

She ignored him.

"That'd suit me just fine," he yelled. "But that's not how this is going to go."

She stopped in her tracks and whirled around.

"What? What do you mean?"

"Speak to your solicitor, Rose," Joe called. "Just speak to your solicitor."

"How about *you* speak to *your* solicitor, Joe Fraser," she yelled, stepping under her porch, shedding her wet layers.

"How about *you* speak to *your* solicitor!"

Chapter Fourteen

Rose felt the colour drain from her face.

She steadied herself against a towering mahogany bookcase that was stuffed with leather-bound legal tomes.

"Please, Mr Abernethy," she said. "Spell it out for me. I can't be hearing this right."

Hector's solicitor gave her a look that signalled his diminishing patience.

"And in terms that even an idiot would understand, please. Because trust me, I am feeling very much like an idiot right at this moment."

Donal Abernethy peered over the top of his glasses and made a harrumphing sound deep in his throat.

"Once again, Miss Mackie," the solicitor began, even more slowly than his prior efforts that morning, "what I am saying is... The stipulation is for one year."

Rose blinked.

That's what she'd thought he was saying. Only – the whole thing was still incomprehensible. A year. A year on the island. Unless Joe Fraser gave her his seal of approval on the purchaser of the cottage.

"One. Year." Mr Abernethy said again in clear, clipped tones, warming to the idea of her idiocy now. "Twelve. Months. Do you understand? Twelve *calendar* months."

Rose had been variously pacing the room and gripping onto bookcases, but now she simply slumped back down into the buttoned-leather chair across from the solemn, jowly-cheeked executor of Hector's will.

"A year," she said flatly. "A *year*. How can this be right? I can't stay on Primrose Island for a year! I have to work and I have to... I have to..."

Rose stilled, a thought washing into her brain. A question.

What *did* she have to do? Work aside? Why couldn't she stay on this island for a year? If she wanted to? Or even if she was being *made* to?

Mr Abernethy was by now busying himself with the re-pocketing of fountain pens and the shuffling of documents into neat, ribbon-tied stacks.

"Those are the terms, Miss Mackie," he said in a time-to-conclude-this-meeting tone of voice. "Either leave the buyer approval to Mr Fraser, or take up residence in the house, on the island, for the term of one year."

With that, the solicitor took off his glasses and looked at Rose, his face softening a little.

"It's a wee bit unusual, I'll grant you. Nevertheless, Mr Mackie's wishes are to be respected. And the stipulations made in his will are to be carried out."

"If I stayed..."

Woah – what was she even saying? *If* she stayed...? What was that?

"IF I stayed... what would I do, exactly? For a year?"

Mr Abernethy remained silent. Apparently, he didn't know.

"And there's nothing to be done?" Rose said. "Nothing at all?"

The solicitor shook his head. "I'm afraid not. From a legal standpoint, Hector made sure to dot all the 'i's and cross all the 't's. It is what it is, as they say. If you want to sell the house, the ownership of the house has to be legally conferred to you. And for that to happen, well, it seems you're going to have to let Mr Fraser choose the buyer."

"I do *not* want to do that."

"Aye, well, in that case, you'll just have to hunker down on Primrose Island for a good long time."

"And I do *not* want to do that, either."

The morning after meeting with Mr Abernethy, Rose had plodded along the beach to the Gannet's Beak grocery to buy a lemon, only to find herself in a rigorous interview situation with Elspeth McGillicuddy, who was, by all accounts, a contender for the title of Island Matriarch.

"Age?"

"Thirty-six."

"Do you have children?"

"No. No, I don't."

No children.

Mrs McGillicuddy was actually writing this stuff down.

This was getting ridiculous, thought Rose. She'd only come in for a lemon!

"Um, Mrs McGillicuddy?" she politely ventured. "About that lemon? I caught a cold the other night, you see, and I could really do with–"

Mrs McGillicuddy wasn't listening.

"And are you single?" she queried.

"Yes, I mean – I wasn't – until..."

Single, Mrs McGillicuddy wrote neatly in pencil, underneath all the other attributes – or census data, who knew – that Mrs McGillicuddy was determinedly extracting from her.

Yes, it occurred to Rose. *Single.* With everything else that had been going on, she'd had little time to think about that. She and Lawrence had split up three months ago after Rose found out about his cheating... Strange that she had barely thought about it – about him – in all that time.

Single. She was, wasn't she? *She was.*

"Yes. I'm single."

"Good," said Mrs McGillicuddy. "Because let me tell you, we've a fair few eligible bachelors on the island."

Rose resisted the urge to roll her eyes.

"There's David Munro," Mrs McGillicuddy began, "and there's Lockie Anderson and Jasper Struthers... We've lots, Rose, I'm telling you!"

Mrs McGillicuddy pulled a spare till roll from a drawer under the counter, licked her pencil, and started writing men's names on it.

"Mrs McGillicuddy, really, I'm not looking for–"

But Mrs McGillicuddy was deaf to all protests.

"Oh!" she cut in, "and Cameron Fraser! Bit of a tearaway in his younger days. But he seems to have got all that out of his system now. And speaking of the Frasers, let's not forget *Joe* Fraser. No introduction needed there, eh m'dear?"

"Please," said Rose. "Do NOT mention that man's name to me, if you would be so kind."

Mrs McGillicuddy looked genuinely disappointed.

"Oh dear. Some bad blood between you two?"

She put a question mark next to Joe's name, tore off the scrap of till roll paper, and slid it across the counter to Rose.

"You could ask one of these nice young men to take you to the ceilidh," she said matter-of-factly. "Girls do that nowadays, you know."

"Mrs McGillicuddy..." Rose flattened her palms on the counter and took a breath. "First. I haven't come to Primrose Island to date. Second, I'm thirty-six. My *girlhood* is fast becoming a distant memory at this point. And third? I'm just *through* with all that, okay? It's too... it's too *hard*."

Not to mention heart-breaking.

Mrs McGillicuddy was assessing Rose carefully. She leaned a little closer, narrowing her eyes. "There was someone, wasn't there?" she said. "There was someone. And you loved him. And he cheated on you, didn't he? With someone you thought was a friend."

Rose blinked. "A good friend, actually," said Rose. "How did you know that?"

Mrs McGillicuddy gave a small sad shrug of her shoulders. "Because you've the look about you, dear."

"The look?"

"Yes, dear. The look of a scorned woman."

"I *have?*"

What was a scorned-woman 'look', anyway? Mad, staring eyes? A bit... unhingey? Scruffy-yet-beloved cardigans? Tick, tick and tick, if so.

"Yes, dear. You have. Ask me how I know that?"

"Okay, um, how do you know that, Mrs McGillicuddy?"

"Because, Rose, I *too* am a scorned woman. And it takes one to know one. Yes..." Mrs McGillicuddy looked off into the middle distance. "Angus, my husband of twenty-five years, took himself off to a stained-glass workshop in Edinburgh last summer, and pocketed an extra-marital affair while he was at it."

"Oh," said Rose. "I'm sorry."

Mrs McGillicuddy sighed and nodded. "Hence the need for this," she added, whisking aside a curtain to the rear and a little offset from the serving counter to reveal a stately-bosomed dress form draped in tweed.

Rose looked from Mrs McGillicuddy to the tweed-draped mannequin – and back to Mrs McGillicuddy again. "I'm not sure I follow?"

"It's a *revenge* dress, dear. And I'll be wearing it to the ceilidh on Friday night because I know Angus will be attending."

Mrs McGillicuddy swished the curtain back across. "And unless you find yourself an eligible date before then – you, my girl, are coming with me."

"Wh–? Huh?"

Mrs McGillicuddy whipped out a tape measure and rounded the counter in the blink of an eye, and before Rose knew what was happening, the woman had looped it around Rose's bust, and then her waist.

"Uh-huh. Standard size 10," she murmured, more to herself than to Rose.

"Mrs McGillicuddy, please! I only came in for a lemon and–"

The over-door bell tinkled, cutting off Rose's protest, and both women turned to see who was coming through it.

Ugh. No. *Him.*

"Speak of the devil!" Mrs McGillicuddy beamed. "We were just chatting about you, Joe."

Rose's cheeks flamed. "*You* were, Mrs McGillicuddy. *I* wasn't."

"Morning, Elspeth," said Joe, all blue-eyed smiles, adding then, "Morning, Rose."

He strolled towards them. "Chatting about me, eh?" he said, folding his arms, quirking a brow. "I see..."

Rose actually did roll her eyes now. She turned back to face Mrs McGillicuddy. She would not stand here and contribute to the further inflation of the man's ego.

"I really do need that lemon now, please."

Mrs McGillicuddy ignored her.

"Rose here's been telling me her tale of woe, Joe," she said, her hands going to her hips. "Seems her ex-boyfriend was the cheating kind. Seems he betrayed her good and proper. With one of her best friends, to boot."

"Oh for goodness' sake," Rose muttered.

This was too much.

"Okay, I have to go," she said abruptly, turning on her heels and marching out of the store. She brushed against Joe as she did so – the space in the Gannet's Beak store being somewhat limited – and she felt a dozen rebellious butterflies take flight in her tummy.

"Rose," Joe said, by way of acknowledgement, that smile of his now replaced by an expression that could only be described as kind. Concerned, even.

"Joe," Rose muttered by way of reply, trying to keep her eyes looking straight ahead, rather than at him.

Those butterflies. Again.

Once outside, she marched along the beach, feeling the general mix of tension and discombobulation that seemed to accompany all thoughts – and all proximity – to Joe Fraser, dissipate a little with each determined stride.

It was low tide, and the huge expanse of fine pale sand ahead of her glittered with little shards of shell and sea glass. She took it all in. The island's big sky. The turquoise blue of the sea. The cold, sea-salt air. It was all so beautiful, and it occurred to her – all the hassle and confusion of the past week aside, it was going to be hard to leave.

It was going to be hard to leave the *beach*, that was, and the beach *house*. It was going to be hard to leave *them*.

She sneezed, suddenly, and scrabbled in the pockets of her cardigan for a tissue.

She *really* wished she'd managed to get that lemon.

Chapter Sixteen

There was a bang at the door. Coll lifted one ear, and then returned to his slumber on the rug beside the wood burner.

Rose padded down the hall and opened it and...

Butterflies.

...It was Joe. Holding up a lemon.

"Got a cold?" he said, brushing past her, apparently no longer in need of an invitation.

"No," Rose said, immediately following it up with a sneeze.

Joe shot her a sideways look and raised a brow at her.

"I see. Well, I'm going to make you something for your not-cold. Sit down over there by the fire."

Rose opened her mouth to protest, but suddenly her limbs felt even weaker, and instead, she just did as she was told.

From the deep comfort of her fire-side armchair, she watched Joe fill the kettle, then root around in a cupboard until he'd retrieved a jar of heather honey and a three-quarters full bottle of Scotch.

Next, he rummaged in a drawer and pulled out a small glass lemon squeezer.

"There is no cold on earth that cannot be helped out the door by a decent hot toddie," he called over to her from the stove.

And moments later, he was beside her.

"Here," he said, handing her a mug of hot-lemon goodness.

"Thank you," Rose said. "I really *really* wanted this."

"Aye. I could tell."

There was a different feeling to this moment between the two of them. For her part, Rose felt too wobbly and lightheaded to spar with him. But Joe, too, seemed to have parked his combative style for the time being.

He knelt on the rug beside the now-dozing Coll.

"How are you doing, Rose?" he said. "Apart from your cold, I mean. How are you doing, here, in Hector's house?"

Rose ventured a shy look at him. "I'm doing... okay, I guess? But also... I'm finding it a lot."

She took another sip of the heathery lemony whisky-laced toddie.

"Yeah," Joe said quietly. "I can imagine. It *is* a lot. And I'm just – I'm just sorry. That you're dealing with it all. So if I can help... I mean, I know you probably don't want my help... But, if I can do anything, let me know. Okay?"

Rose smiled at him. "Okay, Joe. Maybe I will."

"Right." He stood up, and for a moment, their eyes locked. "See you."

Rose nodded. "See you, Joe," she said. "And thanks." She raised her mug at him in a *Cheers*.

Joe smiled, and gently patted the sleeping Coll before turning towards the door.

"Try and get some rest."

Chapter Seventeen

Rose stirred in the early morning from a long, deep sleep – only to realise it wasn't actually that early.

In fact, it was borderline not the morning anymore.

She stretched, and found herself slowly attuning to a sort of background *thrum*. A background thrum... and the rise and fall of voices.

Chatter, she realised. It could best be described as *chatter*.

Group chatter.

Huh?

She climbed out of bed and padded over to the window. Once the sash was up, she leaned out as far as she safely could to see what was going on.

A queue of people. There was a queue of people – starting at her front door with none other than Joe Fraser – and snaking quite some way down the beach.

Once again: *huh?*

"Well?" Joe called up to her, grinning. "Are you going to let us in? Lot of folk here wanting to see the house."

Folk? Wanting to see the house?

Ah. She got it. He'd been charm itself yesterday morning – all honey and lemon and whisky and kind words. And what had that been in aid of?

It was obvious.

He'd been softening her up. For this. His pincer move.

But wait. All this was making her head hurt.

Wasn't that the *plan?* Shouldn't she be *thanking* him? After all, the greater the number of prospective buyers through the door, the greater the likelihood that Joe would approve one of them, right?

And if she had a buyer, she wouldn't need to spend a moment longer on the island than was necessary. Right?

She pushed away from the window and stood glumly in the middle of the bedroom.

Right.

So why did her heart feel so heavy?

That was the problem with hearts, Rose mused, throwing open the front door of the beach house and allowing the queue of would-be purchasers to stream inside. Hearts couldn't be trusted. Hearts tended not to get it right.

Not in her experience, anyway.

The head though? The head had a lot going for it. Facts. Parameters. Rationality. Sense. These were her life rafts. These were the things she must cling to. Facts... parameters... rationality... and sense. This was, after all, her usual modus operandi. And it had served her well.

Only, not really, cut in a contradictory voice inside her supposedly rational and facts-loving head.

The trouble with you is, the voice prattled on, *you don't listen to your heart nearly enough.*

"Shhh!"

"Who are you shushing?"

Rose whirled around. *Joe.*

She put her hands on her hips. The facts. Stay with the facts.

"You wasted no time, I see."

Joe hooked his thumbs into his belt loops and took a step closer to her to allow another prospective buyer to bustle past.

"Aye. Well. Time wasting's not for me. If you know what I mean."

Rose narrowed her eyes. Instinctively she understood there was a double meaning tangled up somewhere in those words.

But she was in no mood to go looking for it.

Or too cowardly? offered the contradictory inner voice again.

She ignored the taunts being waged against her inside her own head, and instead pulled two small notebooks from one pocket and two pens from another.

She handed one of each to Joe.

"Here. Take notes. It'll help us later. When we're narrowing things down."

Joe glanced over his shoulder at the ever-lengthening queue, and back to Rose again.

And then he smiled.

"Aye. Okay."

It had been a long day. A *loooong* day.

And he'd noticed something. Over the course of it, Rose had gone from almost reluctant-seeming – in terms of having people wander the house, sizing it up for a potential purchase – to, well, quite enthusiastic.

What was that about?

His hunch was that she was in some sort of quandary. Part of her wanted to sell. And part of her, he was beginning to think, might be wondering about not selling.

Whatever the truth may be, for Hector's sake, he needed to stay on task. Which for today, at least, meant an honest thumbs-up or thumbs-down for each and every would-be buyer.

She was tired. He could tell.

"Sure you want to do this tonight?" he said.

Rose nodded, and sat down at the kitchen table. She motioned for Joe to do the same.

"Right," she said. "I've made a list of the people I think are most likely to make an offer. So let's just go through them one by one."

Joe spread his hands. "Fine by me."

Rose cleared her throat.

"Jilly and Gerald Ruskin," she began. "Would you sell to them?"

Joe folded his arms. "Nope," he said. "They just want to do a few repairs on the cheap, then flog it to the highest bidder. I believe they call it flipping. So, again, a strong *no* from me on those two."

Rose tore the page from her notebook, crumpled it, and threw it in the direction of the wastepaper basket.

"These guys, then," she said, tapping the page where she'd scrawled some names and a few relevant details. "Phil and Stan," she offered. "Seemed nice enough?"

"Aye. Nice guys who want to tear the place down and build something – and I quote, 'Bigger, brasher, better'. Another *no*.

Scrunch. Wastepaper basket.

"Eleanor and Patrick," Rose offered.

"Tearing up the machair out the back? Putting down AstroTurf? Sacrilege! No way."

They continued this way for hours. Rose offering more and more contenders, each less promising than the last, before closing her notebook and dropping her head into her hands.

"I think I'd like to stop now," she said. "I can't lie. Today was awful."

It was true. It *had* been awful. There was no way she could bear the thought of *any* of those people buying the house.

In fact, she hated the idea of changing a single thing about it. What was that all about? She hadn't even been able to face taking pictures off the walls, or boxing up any of the quirky ornaments and vases that Hector had acquired over the years.

* * *

Joe frowned. Unless he was very much mistaken, there were tears in Rose's eyes.

He got to his feet and crossed the room to where she was standing.

"It's just..." she was palming away her tears, her eyes going all around the lovely wood-panelled room. "...I don't think I could bear it if anyone tore this place apart. It's all I've got that connects me to..."

Her voice cracked. "Never mind," she said, turning away from Joe. "It's okay."

"Rose," Joe said quietly, moving closer. "Do you *want* to sell this house?"

"Yes. No. I don't know! I just want... I just wish..."

She started to sob quietly, and as she sobbed, words tumbled out of her. Feelings tumbled out of her that she hadn't even known were there...

"Hector wanted," she sobbed, "what was best for the house and best for the island. And you," she sobbed, "want what's best for the house, and best for the island."

"Even I," she sucked in several breaths, trying to get the words out, "... even *I* want what's best for the house and best for the island," she turned to face Joe then. "But, the thing is, no one wants what's best for *me*."

Rose began to turn away again, but Joe put his hands gently on her shoulders and looked at her intensely. "Rose," he said. "What if you stayed?"

His words were quiet. His eyes steady. And his heart, if he were being completely honest, was cut through by a tentative shard of hope that he had not, he realised, allowed himself to feel for a very, very long time.

Chapter Twenty

What if she stayed?

Rose went very still. "But what would I... What would I even *do* here, Joe? If I stayed?"

Joe looked at her for a long moment. "Come on," he said.

"What?"

"I said, come on..."

"Yes, but, come on *where?*"

"To meet a friend of mine," said Joe. "She's been looking after Sam today."

Joe got to his feet. "Come on," he said again, smiling warmly, stirring those butterflies. "And bring your camera."

A suggestion? A *command?* Unclear.

Nevertheless – and without enough time to establish whether her head was in charge at that moment, or whether her heart had taken the reins – Rose grabbed her SLR and her cardigan, and darted after him.

Tilladrum House was a huge Scots Baronial mansion presiding grandly over its own loch and generously smothered in twisting, twining layers of hundred-year-old wisteria.

"The Struthers have lived at Tilladrum – the big house, as we lesser mortals call it – oh, for a couple of hundred years at least," Joe said. "But for posh folk, they're reasonably normal."

And then he grinned. "Reasonably," he said again, smiling broadly as a tomboyish-looking woman about the same age as Rose began striding across the lawn to greet them.

"That right, Freya?" Joe called to her. "You lot are reasonably normal?"

The woman laughed and wrapped her arms around Joe, hugging him tight.

"You know full well there's no one remotely normal around here, Joe Fraser," she said. "And that's how we like it."

Freya turned to Rose and stuck her hand out.

"Hello," she beamed. "I'm Freya."

The two women shook hands warmly.

"Freya, meet Rose," said Joe. "Rose, meet Freya."

Joe then put his hands on his hips.

"Right. Are you lot still needing a photographer?"

Chapter Twenty-Two

While Joe entertained Sam outside, Freya showed Rose around the house's beautiful interior, and also the gorgeous barn that the family used for their wedding venue business.

She talked about all the weddings they handled – which was *a lot* – and how amazing it would be to have a photographer of their own. Someone based on the island.

Ideas and possibilities of a shape previously unimaginable to Rose began to form in her mind.

And maybe also in her heart.

Before Freya left to catch the boat to the mainland, she left Rose and Joe a big heap of tartan picnic blankets to spread in front of the house, and she also pulled together a hasty, though no less delicious for it, afternoon picnic.

"It's lovely here," said Rose, later, hugging her knees, watching Sam play with Coll. "It's just lovely. And Freya's great."

Joe, who'd been lying quietly watching the clouds float by, turned onto his side and propped himself up on one elbow.

He smiled at her. Rose smiled back.

And for that moment, that was enough.

In fact, Rose realised, taking in Joe's kind, handsome face, and feeling *those* butterflies again – it was more than enough. It was perfect.

Well, almost perfect. Because the next thing Rose knew, her phone was ringing loudly and insistently. And when she plucked it from her bag and looked at the caller ID on the screen, her heart sank into her boots.

Lawrence. Her ex.

Chapter Twenty-Three

Where the afternoon had been bright sunshine, tonight – even inside the cosy creaking walls of the beach house – Rose was being buffeted by the wildest storm she'd ever experienced.

The waves crashing against the rocks on the beach below felt perilously close, and rain battered relentlessly against the suddenly fragile-seeming sash windows in great pelts, like handfuls of rice.

"Expect a wee bit of weather tonight," Mrs McGillicuddy had said earlier when Rose had wandered along to the Gannet's Beak to pick up a few essentials. "Wee bit of a hoolie coming in, so get your hatches battened down, m'dear. It'll have blown on by come the morning."

Fair enough, Rose thought, walking the stretch of beach back to the house. The same logic, or wisdom, she realised, could be applied to life – could it not?

She added two more logs to the wood burner, and settled into the deep armchair next to it with Coll at her feet.

Reluctantly, she pulled out her phone. She still hadn't looked properly at any of Lawrence's messages.

"Miss you babe. Call me."

"Rose, could you call me? I've left three messages."

"I'd REALLY appreciate it if you would call me, Rose. Like, NOW."

She sighed. If she responded to *any* of Lawrence's barrage of voicemails and text messages, she'd be creating an opening for him to press on with his self-described *getting-her-back* campaign.

On the other hand, if she ignored all the messages, he might do something unpredictable. And sometimes, Lawrence's *unpredictability* scared her.

Something she'd noticed, though. The longer she spent in this old creaking beach house, and the longer she spent on Primrose Island, the further away Lawrence, and all the complications that came with him, seemed to be.

And Rose found she rather liked that.

She crouched in front of the wood burner and stoked the fire a little.

Then she wandered to the small tray where Hector had kept a few bottles and some upturned glasses.

There was a bright green bottle – a ten-year-old malt. Laph... *Laphro...* La-*what?*

"How do you pronounce this?" she called over her shoulder to Coll.

Coll offered a low *ruff* by way of reply.

"Laph-ro-aig?" she said, sounding out the syllables.

"Literally no idea," she murmured, holding the bottle up to the light to get a better look at it.

"Okay. Well, I've no idea if I'm saying your name correctly, *Laph-ro-aig*, but I'm prepared to sample your wares, nevertheless."

She poured herself a scant measure and held it up in a toast to the room.

Whoa. *Potent*. A little medicinal. And very peaty.

She screwed up her face a bit and again addressed Coll. "I mean, I could *get* to like it? I think? Probably?"

Coll offered an approving *ruff*.

Glass in hand, she went room to room upstairs to check the latches on the windows.

The wind – or the *hoolie*, as Mrs McGillicuddy had put it – was battering the little house mercilessly.

The last of the rooms she entered was Hector's study. She stood in the doorway for a long moment.

This old creaking beach house in the Hebrides had been bequeathed to her – well, in theory, anyway – by a man who'd spent the best part of forty years actively ignoring her. And when she was alone, when she ran this fact again and again through her consciousness, it just... didn't add up.

Maybe none of it added up. This house, and her *in* it. This island, and her *on* it.

She took another sip of the whisky and glanced at her watch. Was it too late to phone Callie?

Callie was her agent back in London, and if she called Callie, if she let Callie talk to her for long enough, she'd get her mind back on work.

Back on the cold hard facts.

Hector hadn't wanted her.

The house wasn't really – shouldn't really – be hers.

And as much as it had been a charming little daydream for five minutes earlier that day? Her work – her *life* – wasn't on this island. Was it?

Perhaps it could be, though? If you'd let it?

Her contradictory heart talking again.

She *shushed* it, and walked further into Hector's study, squinting into the darkness to make out the desk lamp.

From somewhere far away over the sea came another long, low rumble of thunder.

Squeezing her way out of a dark corner, having fumbled into it accidentally in trying to locate the lamp switch, Rose knocked her shin against something hard.

"Ow!" she yelped. It was one of the desk drawers. She'd knocked it, and its contents, onto the floor. "Ow, ow, ow, ow, *ow!*"

She sucked in some air and bit hard on her lip, fumbling now in a more promising corner for the lamp switch, bracing herself for the sight of her mangled leg.

Click

And then – in the newly illuminated space – she froze.

Letters.

Dozens of them.

Strewn across the rug – each one with her name on it, penned in a lovely, old-fashioned hand: *Rose*

She stood there for an age just staring at them, staring at how her name, *Rose*, was penned over and over and over again on countless ivory envelopes.

Finally, slowly, she picked one of them up and turned it over in her hands.

It wasn't sealed.

Chapter Twenty-Four

She went very still, and slid out the contents.

My dear Rose,

Rain today. Good Lord, a deluge of it. Found myself wondering where you might be this week. Last I heard you were in Mexico City. Mexico City! I think I have finally lost count of the number of cities you've been to, Rose. Lately, I find myself wondering if you ever get tired of it? All those hotels and aeroplanes? But saying that, no doubt you've a streak of the tumbleweed in you. I'd say your mother did, too.

She picked up another at random:

My dear Rose,

Today I decorated what I like to call the room with the view. I chose rambling-rose wallpaper. Rambling Rose – well, that's you, isn't it? It goes nicely with an old quilt my mother made. Now, of course, I'm an old bachelor, and I don't know a thing about making a room look pretty. But if I say so myself, it looks quite cosy. I wonder if we'll meet one day, Rose. I wonder if you'll ever come and tell me what you think of these old rambling roses.

And another:

My dear Rose,

Got myself a dog today. Or, more's the case, a dog got himself me. Found him wandering up at the wee glen. Skin and bone, he is. And nobody on the island can place him. Looks like he hasn't eaten in a month. He's a wee collie, so of course I'm calling him Coll. I think we're going to be friends.

Rose looked up and stared into the middle distance.

He *wrote* to her. Her father *wrote* to her?

Her heart was hammering in her chest. Her cheeks wet, her throat squeezed shut. All these letters... He'd written them... Her father had written them – to *her.*

Fresh tears spilled from her eyes. Her chest constricted. Thirty-odd years of questions, anger, resentment dissolving in one overwhelming moment. Telescoping into a single thought:

He'd cared. He had *cared.*

Rose swallowed an enormous sob, and what remained of the *Laphroaig*, then carefully gathered together every single one of the precious envelopes, and sank cross-legged with them to the floor.

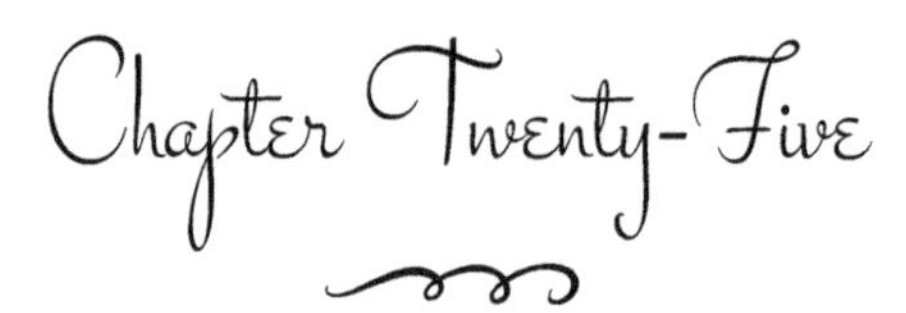

Chapter Twenty-Five

It was morning.

The storm had passed.

Rose jolted awake from a fitful sleep, and the first thing she registered was her breathing.

It was too fast.

Her heart was hammering against her ribcage, her pulse thrumming in her ears.

Was it a panic attack? A *heart* attack?

Then, from nowhere, tears...

She sat up and felt her breath hitch. Had to suck in a big, desperate swallow of air. And this was followed by sobs. The kind of sobs that had never come out of her before. Strangled, desperate, convulsive sobs. Sobs that were all tangled up with her father's letters and her mother's deception. With a never-ending succession of hotel rooms and Joe Fraser's family table. With diva models and lovable old dogs.

It was a mess. *She* was a mess.

She couldn't fully grasp what exactly she was crying about. She didn't even care. She just knew that she needed to cry. Needed to purge this terrible sense of loss. This terrible, aching sadness.

When the house phone rang an hour later, Rose was sitting in bed, hugging her knees, her cheek resting on her arms, her tears spent.

"Hello?" Her voice was hoarse.

"Rose? Hi sweetie, it's me."

"Callie, hi." Rose smiled. Callie. She must have picked up her voicemail.

"Were you sleeping? Want me to call back later?"

"No. No, it's fine. I'm awake. It's good to talk to you."

"Good to talk to me? Are you okay? You usually groan when I wake you up."

Rose laughed. That wasn't entirely untrue.

"So, I got your message, Callie said. "Not that you gave much away. How's it going in the wilds of Scotland?"

"Yeah... It's going okay. I mean, it's a bit strange, to be honest. I'm in my father's house, and–

"Cool-cool-cool."

Callie wasn't listening.

"Listen," her friend continued, her words pouring out at breakneck speed, "and I'm sorry, but I have to be quick... I need to talk to you about a commission. A really exciting commission. A really, really *big* commission."

Rose closed her eyes.

"Rose... Rose? Are you still there?"

"Yes. I'm here. Callie...?"

"Yeah?"

"I think I'm homesick..."

Callie uttered an expletive.

"Okay. Rose? Two things. First of all, you've been on that island for the blink of an eye. Seriously. You can't possibly be homesick. Secondly, you don't have a home, well not one you use, anyway. So I repeat. You can't possibly be homesick."

Callie had a point. Callie had two points, in fact.

How can you be homesick if you don't have a home?

"Anyway, get this," Callie rattled on. "Rolf Van der Mer, Rose. Rolf Van der Mer wants you to art-direct his next shoot. Said he'll only go with you on this one. Said to name your fee. Can you believe it? You're going to have to catch the next flight out. He's going to put you up in his personal penthouse on the Champs-Elysées, then fly you from Paris to Los Angeles in his private jet. This is it, Rose. Rolf Van der Mer. We're talking major league. I'll call the people in Madrid, okay? I'll cancel the Cava job and I'll bump everything else that's bump-able. You just get your stuff together, and get on a plane."

Rose was staring at the wallpaper in the room she'd fallen asleep in last night, tracing the pattern lightly with her index finger.

Rambling roses.

She'd fallen asleep in this room last night. She smiled, tucking the phone under her chin while she slid out of bed and padded over to the window to watch the sun come up. The beach below was strewn with shells and seaweed and driftwood. The aftermath of the storm. It had picked everything up and set it back down again wildly. Differently.

She smiled at the thought. Hashtag: *strongrelate*, Callie would say.

She stayed there for a long moment watching the sun do its work, feeling the first tentative rays of light reach into the bedroom.

"Rose? Rose? So I'll confirm then, yes?"

Callie's voice filtering through again.

A sudden feeling of calm washed over Rose.

A heady sort of lightness.

A strong and quiet certainty that she knew what she was doing.

"No," she said.

"Huh?" said Callie. "What?"

"No, Callie," Rose said again. "I'm not coming. Tell Van der Mer I can't do it. Tell him I have other commitments."

Rose knew what was coming, and she held the phone away from her ear while Callie shrieked manically down the line.

"Are you insane? You can't tell Rolf Van der Mer *No*! Listen, Rose, I don't know what's happening to you out there in haggis-country, but *please*. Please don't do this. This is everything you've worked for. Don't sabotage it now. Don't–"

"I can't, Callie. I'm sorry. I need to..."

What? *What* did she need?

And then it came to her.

"I need to be here."

"Wait. A minute ago you said you were homesick!"

"I think it's *here* that I'm homesick for. That I've *always* been homesick for. This house. This island. The people who live here..."

It took saying it to know that it was true. *Here*. Primrose Island. It was home.

"Don't you dare hang up!" Callie shouted. "We need to talk this through!"

"Call you tomorrow," said Rose. "Promise."

Rose shut off her phone, and breathed.

She dropped it onto the dinky bedroom chair, and returned her attention to the view. This was, after all, the *room with the view*. Sea and sky. Sun and clouds. She was so used to snapping up a hotel blind in the morning and seeing buildings and cars, and... more buildings. You could forget, spending all your time in cities, that a raw, elemental place like this actually existed. She lifted up the sash and took a long, deep breath of the clean, storm-scrubbed air.

She'd read for hours last night. Scores of Hector's letters. She'd laughed and she'd cried. Over the little details of his life. And over his deepest, most heartfelt thoughts and hopes and dreams and sorrows.

Like being kept apart from her. *Away* from her. And how her mother's family had employed expensive lawyers to keep it that way. She'd cried bitter tears about that.

But the more of the letters she read, the more Hector, her father, came alive to her. She heard his *voice*. For the first time in her life, she got to *know* him.

It made her smile to get a sense of what the island meant to him. The place and the people. The simple life he'd had.

He'd been happy.

The thought came to her now quietly, simply, surely. It mattered to her, the knowledge that he'd been happy. And she suddenly knew just as surely that *her* happiness had mattered to *him*. They'd never met, and now they never would. But they shared blood. They shared a past. They shared a bond. And she would hang on to that, always. Even if she couldn't change the past, or repair what they'd both lost, maybe she could make it all mean something.

Maybe she could give her father that.

Maybe she could give *herself* that.

She turned away from the window and walked slowly downstairs to the kitchen. While she waited for the coffee to brew, she pulled out and unfolded the last letter of Hector's that she'd read, which was also, she now knew, the last one he wrote.

My dear Rose,

I'm not much for words. Lord knows, I'm no great talker. Some folk call me a bit of an old curmudgeon. Aye. That may be true. I'm more of a grump than a philosopher, in any case. But I've picked up a crumb or two of experience along the way. And Rose, what I would say to you is this: You can't unscramble an egg. And I've learned over time that this often turns out to be a good thing. Be happy in your life, Rose. Don't worry about the broken things, or the messy things, or the things that seem unfixable. It might turn out to be that they're not. Fixable, that is. Make your peace with those broken, scrambled things – with all those scrambled eggs – and see if you can find a way to enjoy them. Because life is full of surprises, Rose. This wee island, Rose, is full of surprises – and I'd love for you to find that out one day.

I don't know how much longer I've got, Rose. So I'm saying goodbye. And I'm telling you that I love you.

Yours always,

Hector. Your father.

Chapter Twenty-Six

Rose had spent the day in her pyjamas sipping coffee and re-reading every single one of Hector's letters to the point where *all cried out* was something she now understood to be a very real thing.

She guessed it must be early evening when she heard loud insistent banging on the front door.

"Rose! Rose? It's Elspeth McGillicuddy! I'm here to take you to the ceilidh!"

Ceilidh? What ceilidh?

What even was a ceilidh?

Rose creaked the door open, and Elspeth McGillicuddy's jaw fell open.

"My goodness me, the state of you!" she said. "What on earth's happened?"

Rose preferred not to imagine what she must look like. Red-rimmed eyes, mussed up hair, her raggedy old cardigan hauled over an even *more* raggedy sleep t-shirt.

"Never mind. We don't have time. Go back inside, dear. That's it. That's right. In with you and up the stairs," Mrs McGillicuddy said in her sing-song voice. "You're having a bath, and you're putting on a dress, and you're coming to the ceilidh with me."

Rose protested weakly. "I can't, Mrs McGillicuddy. I don't have a dress..."

"Yes you *do* have a dress, young lady," Mrs McGillicuddy fired back. "And not just any dress, either."

The woman at that point reached deep into a heavily embroidered carpet bag and pulled out an incredibly pretty fluttery-silk tea dress.

"*This* dear," she said, "*this* is a revenge dress. And I made it for you myself."

"You did?" said Rose, genuinely touched, fresh tears filling her eyes. "You made it for *me?*"

"Uh-huh. Now come on! Chip-chop up the stairs! Let's get you in a bath," she said briskly, and then, far more quietly, and very, very gently, "... and let's get those tears washed away."

Chapter Twenty-Seven

Two hours later, Elspeth McGillicuddy hooked Rose's arm through her own, and proudly walked her into one of the island's famous ceilidhs.

Various women, and quite a few men, flocked around them, *oohing* and *ahhing* at Elspeth's impressive sewing skills.

And that's when Rose felt a tap on her shoulder.

"Hello."

She turned around.

Of course.

That tap. That flat-toned voice. And that tight, put-out expression.

Lawrence.

Lawrence made a long head-to-toe sweep of Rose in her fluttering floral tea dress. And, not for the first time, Rose registered his gaze as an uncomfortable combination of withering and sleazy.

"Lawrence," she said quietly. "What are you doing here?"

She saw tension, a particular tautness in his jaw. He was angry with her. *He* was angry with *her*.

"Well," he began, "you've ignored my calls, voicemails, texts, WhatsApps and emails..." he was counting off each one on the fingers of one hand. "And, I mean, I could've written you a letter I suppose. But in the end, I thought it'd be fun to drop in to your little backwater in the Hebrides and see what you were up to."

Rose hadn't really noticed until that moment how cold Lawrence's eyes could be.

"See what I'm up to?" she repeated. "To be honest, Lawrence, whatever it is I'm *up* to, as you put it, is frankly no longer any business of yours."

"Oh, I think it is, Rose," he hissed. "Come outside. I want to talk to you."

Lawrence gripped her elbow tight – too tight – and made to steer her away from the crowd.

"Don't do that–" she said, trying to pull her arm free.

"Don't make a scene, Rose."

Rose tried again to free her arm.

"You're hurting me. Stop it," she said, yanking her arm free forcefully this time.

And as Rose spun away from Lawrence and his grabbing hands, she collided with the broad chest of a much taller man.

And she was incredibly relieved to find that the chest in question belonged to Joe.

"Rose," he said quietly, looking from her to Lawrence – and back to her again. "Everything all right here?"

"Everything's fine, mate," Lawrence cut in. "We're having a private conversation though? So if you wouldn't mind clearing off?"

Rose interjected now. "We're not having any conversation whatsoever, Lawrence. About anything. Ever again. Go home. It's over. It was over a long time ago."

Lawrence's face twisted, and he grabbed at Rose, roughly.

Chapter Twenty-Eight

That was not acceptable. That was not acceptable *at all.*

"No, no, no, no – no you don't," said Joe, putting himself between Rose and her low-life ex.

"Don't ever do that again," he said. "To Rose. Or to any woman. D'you understand?"

Lawrence gulped and swallowed and nodded and recoiled, shrinking against the wall, understanding suddenly that this gentle giant was not to be messed with.

"Come with me, Rose?" he said, resorting to his whiny, pleading voice now – his last-ditch attempt to get her buy-in. "Please? We can fix this, babe. I know we can."

"No, Lawrence," said Rose, standing beside Joe now, feeling his warmth. His protection. "No. We can't."

And then, with nothing more than a nod of his chin, Joe indicated to Lawrence it was time to start walking.

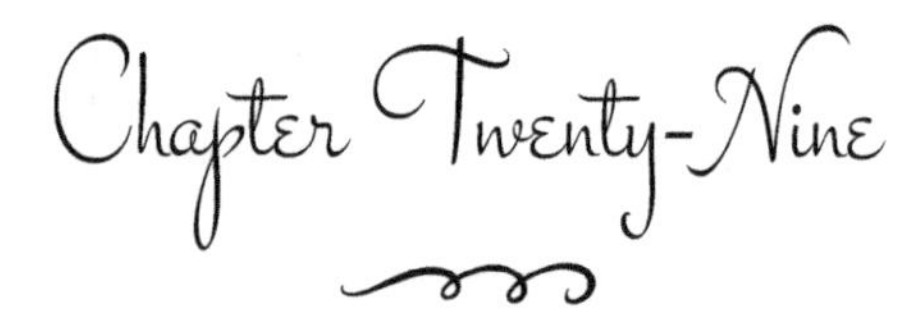

Chapter Twenty-Nine

Rose and Joe watched him go.

And then they walked around the edge of the room to get a better view of the dancing.

Joe handed Rose a glass of the whisky-laced fruit punch. "So," he started up, his eyes twinkling mischief, "...what happened to your cardigan? You know, the one that looks like it went to war against an army of moths. And lost."

Rose laughed at the same time as the rise and swell of the ceilidh jostled the two of them a bit closer.

Butterflies.

"Oh. Thought I'd leave it at home tonight," she shouted over the noise. "Give it a day off."

"Aye? Well that's some dress you've got on," said Joe, leaning in close to make himself heard over the fiddles and the foot stompings, now that the ceilidh was in full swing.

Rose blushed pink.

"Here," Joe reached into his pocket and pulled out a small corsage of heather and some of the blue primroses unique to the island, and for which the island had been named. "I made this for you. In case you turned up."

Rose scanned his face, then helped him pin the corsage to her dress.

She was still scanning his face when he reached for her. The lightest of touches. His fingers brushing hers, then taking her hand in his.

Yet more butterflies.

He looked at her with dark, gentle eyes. "Would you dance with me, Rose?" he said.

And not for the first time with Joe, Rose felt there was a deeper meaning to his words, and that her heart was attuning itself to his. She smiled at him, and leaned still closer.

"Yes, Joe," she said. "I'd love to dance with you."

At that precise moment, Elspeth McGillicuddy, who had been watching Rose and Joe like a hawk for a whole ten minutes, catapulted herself free of *The Dashing White Sergeant* and birled towards them.

There was mischief and matchmaking in her eyes.

"Why don't you two drop in to the Gannet's Beak in the morning?" she trilled over the music and the dancing. "I'll do you both a nice breakfast."

Joe raised a brow, inviting Rose's response.

"Sure," Rose said, smiling widely. "Why not?"

"Good," the older woman beamed. "Give me a wee heads-up then... How d'you both like your eggs?"

Rose smiled at Joe and Joe smiled at Rose.

"I like mine scrambled, Mrs McGillicuddy," Rose said, blinking back a tear, and sending Hector – sending her *dad* – a little burst of love.

"Aye, said Joe," without taking his eyes off Rose. "Scrambled'll do me too," Elspeth. "Scrambled'll do me just fine."

And with that, Joe gathered Rose up into his big strong arms and kissed her – properly – before whirling her off into the heart of the ceilidh.

And Rose understood. *Finally*, she understood. She was, at long last, a Rose who had rambled all the way *home*.

The End

Also by Holly Wyld

♥ **Welcome to Primrose Island!** ♥

Titles in the Primrose Island novellas series:

A Scottish Island Surprise

One Spring at Tilladrum

A Girl Called Brodie

Lara's Lighthouse

The Island Castle

When Freya Met Magnus

♥ THE PRIMROSE ISLAND NOVELLAS ♥

✓ Heartwarming, standalone short stories

✓ Laugh-out-loud romantic comedy

✓ Wildly beautiful Scottish settings

✓ Characters to fall in love with

Perfect for fans of Scottish Highland romantic comedies from Jenny Colgan, Rachael Lucas, Lisa Hobman and Julie Shackman.

Connect with Holly on Facebook!

www.facebook.com/authorhollywyld

Ingram Content Group UK Ltd.
Milton Keynes UK
UKHW040756030723
424469UK00005B/415